S

Illustrated by
Kenneth Lilly

Written by
Angela Wilkes

DORLING KINDERSLEY, INC.
NEW YORK

Contents

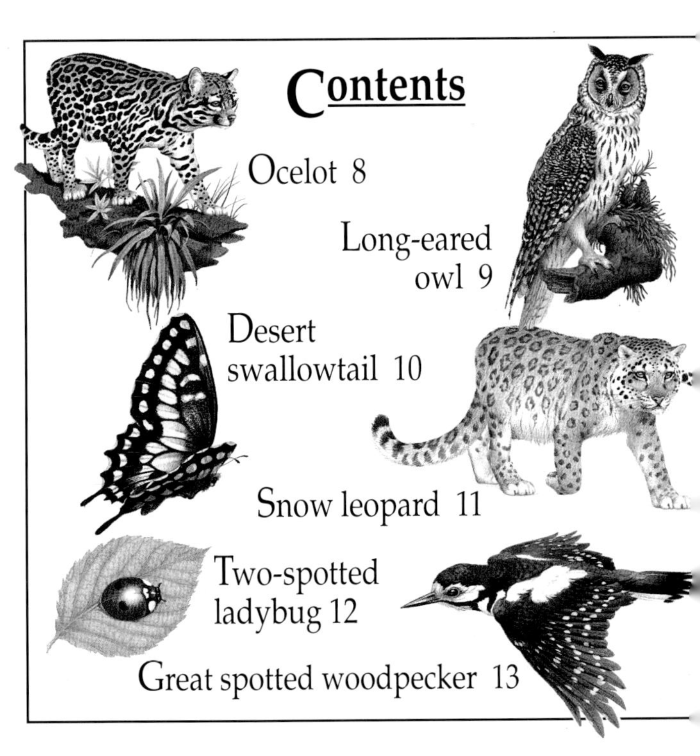

Ocelot 8

Long-eared owl 9

Desert swallowtail 10

Snow leopard 11

Two-spotted ladybug 12

Great spotted woodpecker 13

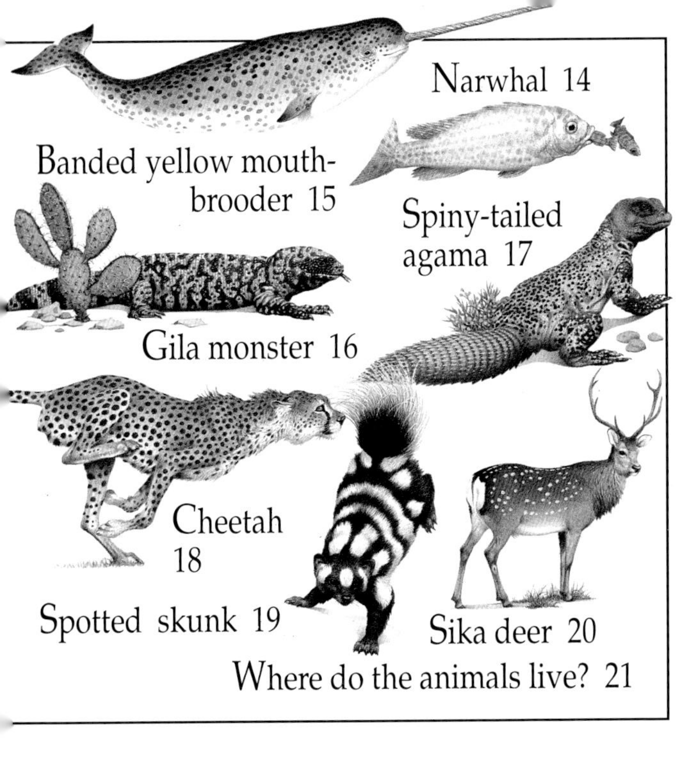

Narwhal 14
Banded yellow mouth-brooder 15
Gila monster 16
Spiny-tailed agama 17
Cheetah 18
Spotted skunk 19
Sika deer 20
Where do the animals live? 21

Ocelot
Every ocelot has different markings on its fur. These beautiful cats are now very rare.

Long-eared owl
The "ears" of this owl are really tufted feathers.

Desert swallowtail
This butterfly is so-named because of its long, pointed wings, which look like a swallow's tail.

Snow leopard
This leopard's spotted fur helps
it slink through snowy mountains
without being seen.

Two-spotted ladybug
A ladybug's hard wing cases protect its soft body. It feeds on small insects.

Great spotted woodpecker
This woodpecker clings on to trees, and uses its sharp beak to dig for insects in the bark.

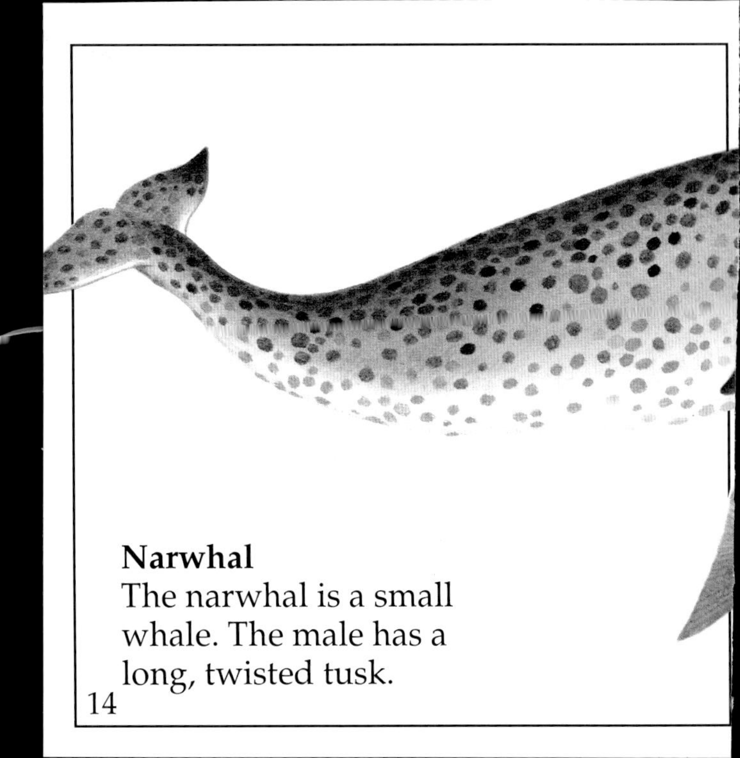

Narwhal

The narwhal is a small whale. The male has a long, twisted tusk.

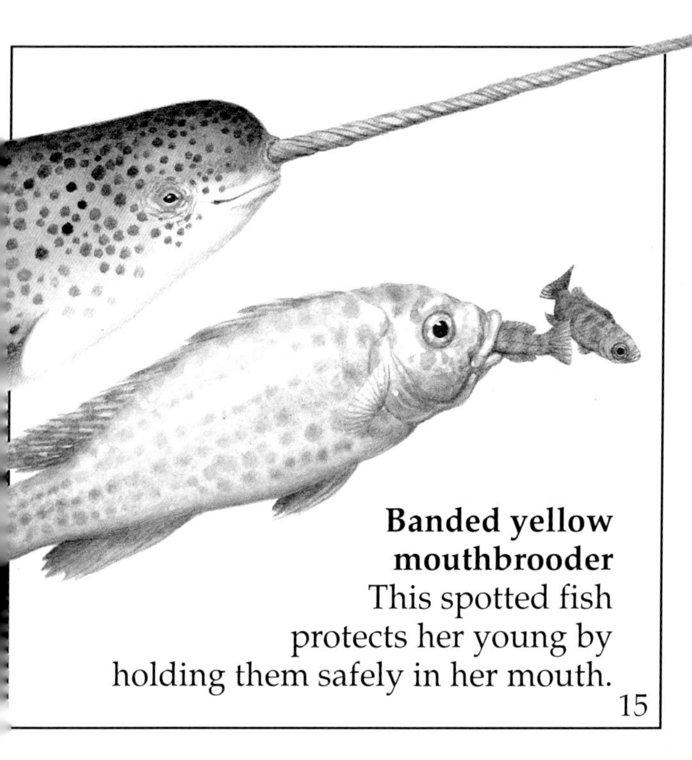

Banded yellow mouthbrooder
This spotted fish protects her young by holding them safely in her mouth.

Gila monster
This lizard's brightly patterned skin warns enemies that it is poisonous.

Spiny-tailed agama
Spotted skin helps this lizard hide in the sand and pebbles of the desert.

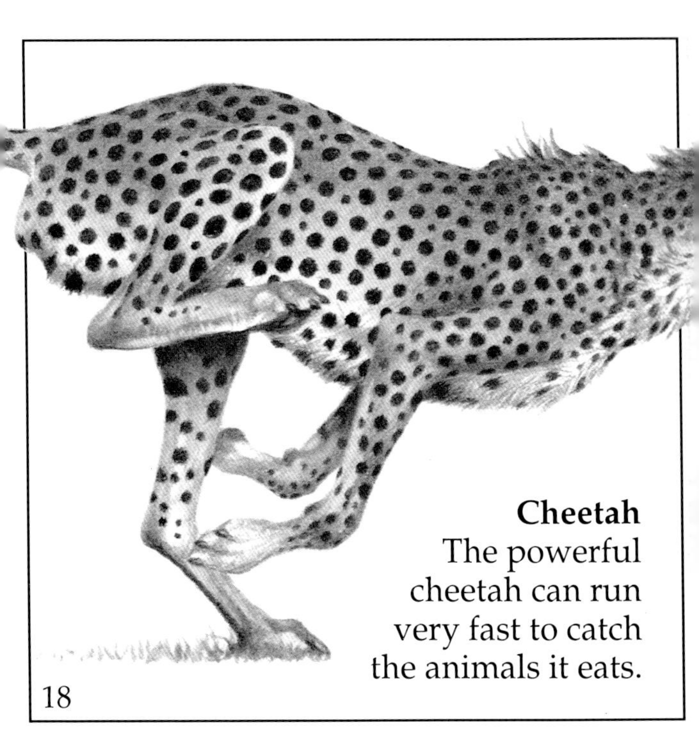

Cheetah
The powerful cheetah can run very fast to catch the animals it eats.

Spotted skunk
This skunk sprays its enemies with smelly liquid to frighten them.

Sika deer

The white spots on this deer's sides hide it among sun-dappled, leafy trees.

Where do the animals live ?

Ocelot
Central America

Long-eared owl
Forests of northern Europe

Desert swallowtail
North American deserts

Snow leopard
Himalaya Mountains

Two-spotted ladybug
Fields and gardens, North America

Great spotted woodpecker
European woodlands

Narwhal
Arctic Ocean

Banded yellow mouthbrooder
Lake Malawi, Africa

Gila monster
North American deserts

Spiny-tailed agama
Sahara desert, northern Africa

Cheetah
African savannah

Spotted skunk
North American deserts

Sika deer
Japanese forests

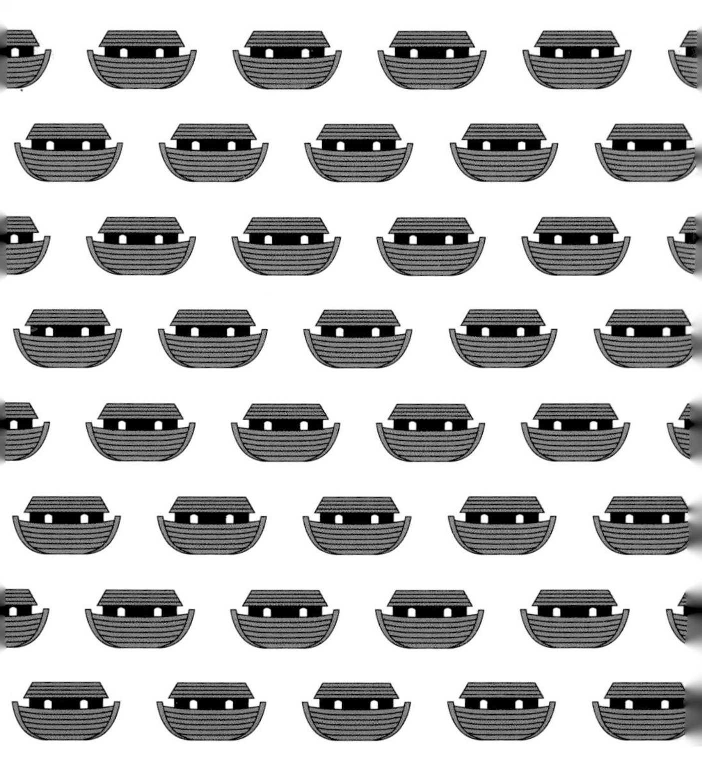